A DISTANT ECHO

The Chris Echo Files

-short story-

TARA MEYERS

ISBN-13: 978-1539893103
ISBN-10: 1539893103

A DISTANT ECHO

Copyright © 2016 Tara Meyers
Forest Grove Books

Cover art design Copyright © Melchelle Designs
http://melchelle.designs.com/

Photographer: Tara Ellis Photography

All rights reserved. No part of this book may be reproduced, stored in a retrieval system, or transmitted by any means without the written permission of the author.

This is a work of fiction. Names, characters, places and incidents either are the product of the author's imagination or are used fictitiously. Any resemblance to actual persons, living or dead, business establishments, events, or locales is entirely coincidental

AUTHORS NOTE

Thank you for purchasing A Distant Echo! This is a short story of around 10,000 words, and is meant as a lead-in to a new, thrilling crime series called The Chris Echo Files. It takes the average reader around one to one-and-a-half hours to read. In it, you will be introduced to CSI, Chris Echo, and get a special view into how things are set up for the first full-length novel, Echo of Fear. Join our newsletter to be notified of all special events and releases: http://eepurl.com/cj_xc

One

Chris Echo was looking at a killer.

Pulling her long mane of brown hair back from her face in frustration, Chris leaned in close to the color 8x10 photo laid out on the desk in front of her. The sharp, intelligent grey eyes that belonged to a finely chiseled face might fool everyone else, but she'd seen his kind before. The business degree, and high paying job gave the impression of stability, but Chris saw beyond the façade.

"If only I could convince Mick of that," Chris mumbled, huffing heavily in frustration.

Mick Walters was her supervisor on the

Crime Scene Investigation (CSI) team. She'd been a member of the elite group in the Seattle, Washington office for just over a year.

Leaning back in the cheap office chair, Chris tore her focus away from the picture of Martin Eastabrooke to gaze at her own framed certificate on the wall. Six years of college earned her the combo criminal justice and psych degree. The Seattle PD had been eager to hire her. She was a needed minority, and spent the next six years 'learning the beat' as a patrol officer, and the last two as a detective. At thirty-two, she now acted primarily as a Criminal Profiler. Examining all the evidence, she'd come up with a list of suspect attributes, and sometimes - even names.

Like now. Unfortunately, the proof on Eastabrooke was all circumstantial, and she'd been unable to give Mick anything more concrete. They were approaching the one-week mark, and Chris knew her leads were going to go cold if she didn't dig up something else *soon*.

Looking back down at the open file, she slid the top photo aside to reveal another, smaller one beneath it. A young, pretty blonde girl with amazing blue eyes hugged the neck of a horse, while smiling sweetly. It was Lisa Emery's senior portrait. Her parents apologized when they gave it to Chris, explaining that it was the most recent image they had of their daughter. She was supposed to graduate the next month, but her parents were burying her that weekend, instead.

Her body was found by a park maintenance crew five days ago, stashed behind a port-a-potty. It was a popular park near the heart of Seattle, and spanned several treed acres. Her parents had no idea why she was there. Although she sometimes went jogging on the weekends, it wasn't a location she was known to visit.

Her time of death indicated she'd been murdered in the early morning hours on Saturday. She'd spent the previous night at her best friend's house, and left there at six am, claiming she had to work. A simple phone call confirmed this, but she wasn't scheduled to be at her department store job until ten am.

During that four-hour gap, someone had stabbed Lisa Emery to death. There were only three wounds, but they were precisely placed in her torso. The official cause of death was internal hemorrhaging, but she'd also received several blows to the head, likely to subdue her. There were no signs of sexual assault, thankfully, but that was little consolation to her freaked-out parents.

She wasn't in jogging gear, and she was wearing makeup. This led Chris to believe that Lisa was meeting someone she didn't want her parents or friends to know about. Chris got the warrant for her cell phone executed a couple of days ago, and there were more than a dozen calls from a burner phone over the past six months, including the night before her murder. No text messages. Whoever it was, didn't want to be found.

Three years ago, Chris was assigned to a case as a detective that was never solved. It involved a thirty-year-old female attorney, apparently mugged and stabbed in the alley behind her townhouse.

Martin Eastabrooke had been one of a small handful of suspects. He and Stephanie Kerns dated briefly the year before, and according to friends, it took Kerns several months and the threat of a restraining order to end it.

The problem was that Stephanie had a habit of dating a lot of men, often at the same time. There had been two other bad breakups that same year, but without any physical evidence at the scene to point to any of them, it was determined to be a random killing. Her purse was rummaged through, money and credit cards stolen, and there were defensive wounds on her hands that indicated she'd fought with her attacker. Everything pointed to Stephanie Kerns being mugged, and when she didn't hand the purse over, it got physical, and she ended up getting stabbed. Case closed.

Until now. Chris pulled the file on Monday, and after Mick gave the okay to re-open it as a possible connection, the first person she brought in for an interview was Eastabrooke. He was just as cool and collected then as he had been before, but her gut was just as certain, too. According to Mick, her gut wasn't enough. The guy was as clean as they come, and claimed to have a solid alibi for the timeframe. She was still waiting for him to produce the ticket for the ferry he was supposedly on that past Saturday morning.

It was hard to verbalize *what* it was about the man that made Chris's skin crawl. In addition to her schooling and personal history, she had an uncanny ability to read people. There was emptiness in Eastabrooke that she'd experienced before, while in the presence of known sociopaths. But there was also something else. Something dark, and sinister.

Tuesday, she started searching the statewide criminal case databases, and by midafternoon, she'd discovered the murder of twenty-four-year-old Kelly Humphry. It was ten years ago, and in a neighboring county. Admittedly, the only similarity was the placement of the puncture wounds but it was enough to justify a comparison. The possibility of a serial killer was nothing to take lightly, and Chris immersed herself in the investigation over the past two days.

Spreading the three thick manila folders across her desk, Chris tapped a pen on the notepad hidden under them. It contained the copious notes she'd made from the case files, and the scribblings that was the product of her latest brainstorming session. She noted the women's names, ages, hair, and eye color. She compared their professions, education, close friends, and public places they frequented. Other than the stab wounds, there was *nothing* similar about them. The only other possible connection was demographics. Lisa and Stephanie were both from King County, in or near Seattle, while Kelly lived in Snohomish County, a half-hour drive north of the city.

"I'm missing something," Chris said to herself, while gathering all the portraits. Three very different women, from eighteen to thirty years old, all brutally attacked and murdered with possibly the same weapon, in the same manner. There had to be a detail she was overlooking. It would most likely entail her going back and re-interviewing all of the people connected to the earlier cases. Every point needed to be scrutinized. If she could get Mick to assign the other profiler, Carlton to it, they might be able to dig through the mountain of information in the next month or two.

A knock on her partially open door caused Chris to jump, and she looked up quickly, already irritated at the intrusion. When she saw Andrew standing there, her irritation grew.

"What?" she demanded, more sharply than the situation warranted.

Cocking his head slightly, Andrew Johns squinted his dark eyes at her. "What's wrong with you?" he asked bluntly, shoving the door wider and entering without an invitation.

Watching him silently as he helped himself to the only other chair in the small room, Chris didn't answer.

"When was the last time you slept?" he pushed. Reclining, he crossed one leg on top of the other.

For some reason, the combination of his tone of voice and relaxed nature pressed yet another of Chris's buttons.

"That's none of your business," she retorted, gathering the folders and thumping them soundly into a neat pile in the center of the desk. The need to appear in control wasn't lost on Chris and her self- psychoanalysis ticked her off even more.

Holding his hands up in a defensive nature, Andrew then uncrossed his leg and leaned forward towards her. "Chris, I just stopped by to let you know that Mick's called for a briefing at nine."

Instantly regretting her anger, Chris closed her eyes briefly while taking a deep, cleansing breath. She knew why she had a strong reaction towards any sort of condescending attitude from Andrew.

He started coming onto her right after she was hired. His dark, handsome good looks and intelligence were both appealing. They'd spent a full month flirting with each other before she noticed the family photos on the desk in his office. Nothing had happened between them, but the humiliation was still intense. Chris fought her whole life to be taken seriously, and being labeled the office tease wasn't how she wanted to start her CSI career. Especially not with a married man.

Things were awkward for a while. Having to trust your team is essential, and Chris felt like she'd been lied to. But while Andrew might be a playboy, he was one hell of an investigator, and Chris came to respect him for his work ethic.

Six months ago, it wasn't a surprise when his marriage failed. Although he'd been single for a while, and he'd tried to ask her out a few times, Chris had no interest in taking him up on his offers. The encounter left a bad taste in her mouth, and she already had relationship issues. It was hard for her to trust. Out of the few serious boyfriends she had, the couple that started talking long term were quickly axed. A couple of them had been real sweethearts and she still felt bad about it, but the others were assholes. Just enough of a balance to keep her convinced that it wasn't worth it.

Peeking up at Andrew from under the hair that fell across her face, Chris did her best to tuck away her bothersome pride. "Thanks," she said as cheerfully as possible. Glancing at the clock on the wall, she saw that the briefing was in five minutes. Standing, she tugged at her stylish black blazer, pulling it down over the edge of her khakis. Forcing herself *not* to continue the primping by messing with her hair, she picked up the documents from her desk and turned back to Andrew.

He was staring at her somewhat intently.

"What?" she demanded, the edge creeping back into her voice.

Slapping at his thighs, Andrew stood abruptly. "Nothing, I guess," he stated, crossing his arms across his broad chest. "If you say you're fine, then you're fine. But I know how hard you push yourself with these cases, Chris. It's not your fault if there simply isn't anything else there to discover."

Picking absently at the corner of her notepad, Chris debated whether she wanted to have this conversation with him. "I know that, Andrew. Really, I do. But it's like I'm looking at a puzzle that I've been working on, and there's that one piece missing that I know had to have fallen on the floor. It's *there*. I'm just not seeing it."

"Take a break," Andrew suggested. "Step away from it for a few days, and maybe you can come at it with a new perspective."

Reaching out, he placed what was supposed to be a comforting hand on her shoulder. A mix of confusing sensations sprang from the contact, and Chris almost ran for the open door, hoping the flush didn't reach her face before she escaped.

Two

"This is your priority for the rest of the week."

Mick slapped the bulging dossier down in front of Chris, on top of the other folders. The briefing had just ended, and Chris was trying to hide both her shock and irritation at the order.

"We have some parents putting their daughter in the ground in two days that might question why," she replied evenly, not looking up to meet his gaze.

Pulling a chair over and straddling it, so that he was facing her, Mick forced her to either look him in the eye, or turn away, which he knew she wouldn't do. "Echo, you're really trying my patience. You're not the only member on this team. I feel that you sometimes forget that. Forensics won't be back until next week, and Katie is still working the autopsy end of it. She should have her preliminary findings on the three comparisons by Monday. Until then, there isn't much else to be done. And this," he added, tapping at the other case, "takes precedence. They need an expert witness, and you've been selected. The hearing is next Thursday, and I need you to have *every* detail in here memorized." Leaning in for emphasis, Mick left no question as to how serious he was. "All of it."

Feeling rightly chastised, Chris chewed at the inside of her cheek. Glancing down at the report, she noticed that it was the horrific domestic violence case from a few months before. It was one of the worse crime scenes she'd ever seen. A mother and two young children were brutally murdered by the mom's boyfriend. He was trying to claim temporary insanity. It was clear, however, that it had all been meticulously planned, and was the act of a sadistic killer. He tried to set-up the kid's father as the suspect, but Chris had pieced it all together, and the forensics confirmed it.

Mick was right; these victims also deserved justice, and she needed to trust the rest of the team to follow the other leads on Lisa Emery's murder. Plus, there was no reason why she couldn't keep up on the rest of the investigation, while preparing for the trial.

"I'm sorry. You're right," she replied, meeting Mick's stare and giving one firm nod. "I'll start on this right away."

"I'm glad you agree," he said evenly, relaxing slightly. Mick paused before continuing. He was always caught off-guard by her unusual gold-green eyes. When they were focused on you, it was intense. "Why don't you work from home for the rest of the day? We both know you would take it with you anyway, and you're much less likely to be … distracted there. In fact," he continued, standing as if the decision were already made, "take one of your comp days tomorrow. HR tells me you're set to lose them again, because you haven't taken a day off yet this year. That's not normal, Chris. Especially since the details of this case might be cause for some of your past ... experiences to be brought up for you. Make it a long weekend, and I'll set up a meeting with forensics on Monday for the testimony."

The only outward sign of Chris's annoyance was the slight flaring of her nostrils. She had no doubt that Andrew must have spoken with Mick. The thought of them conspiring to force her into taking a 'break', was demeaning. For him to throw her 'past' into the mix was a cheap shot at manipulating her compliance.

However, she knew that the only intent behind it was one of concern. While it might be misplaced, it was genuine. There was no harm in going along with it, and as Chris stood, she had to forcefully remind herself to be thankful that she had friends that cared about her wellbeing.

Plus, she would take *all* the files home with her.

***

Chris's cell phone rang as she was pulling

out of the police station parking lot.

Answering it via Bluetooth, she spoke into the air. "Hello, this is Chris Echo."

"Ummm …," a small voice spoke hesitantly. "Is this the investigator I talked to the other day? I'm Emily, Lisa's friend. You gave me your business card, and wrote this number on the back to call you at, if I thought of anything."

Pulling out onto a busy road, Chris squinted in the early afternoon sunshine. It was a rare, warm spring day in Seattle. "No, that's fine. You called the right number, Emily. Do you have something new to tell me?"

Chris recalled the young girl she interviewed at her home on Saturday afternoon. It was hard to get a true impression, given the circumstances. But she seemed like your typical eighteen-year-old teen. Like Lisa, she was a high achiever in school, into sports, and up to her neck in applying for colleges. She took the news of her best friend's death pretty hard, and Chris hoped she might remember something after she'd had a chance to calm down.

"Well, I don't know. I mean, maybe." A heavy sigh echoed through the interior of the car as Emily tried to gather herself. "Last weekend, I stayed at Lisa's. We go – I mean, *used* to go back and forth between our houses." Taking a shuddering breath, Emily sniffed loudly. "So, last weekend, we watched this movie with like, an older guy as the main character. He got with this younger gal, and I was like, 'oooh gross', and Lisa was like, "Why is it gross? I think the guy is kinda hot'."

Chris waited for the story to continue, but as the silence dragged out, she cleared her throat. "Is that it?"

"Well, yeah. Kind of. That might not seem like much, but it was a super weird thing for her to say."

"Do you think she might have been dating an older man that you and her parents didn't know about?" Chris pressed, hoping for more.

"No way. If Lisa were like, *with* a guy, I would have known. But I was thinking about it, and what if she was chatting with some old guy online? What if he talked her into meeting him? Lisa was normally smarter than that, but you never know. I hear about that kind of stuff happening all the time, right? Have you checked her computer?"

Chris took a moment to consider her answer before replying. "I looked at her online activity already, but the forensics team is going over it more thoroughly right now. But Emily, I want you to think about something for me. There were a dozen calls made *to* Lisa's cell over the past several months from a disposable phone. The last four digits were 0028. Does that sound familiar to you? Or can you recall Lisa having any odd conversations that she acted like she didn't want you to hear? Did she ever mention someone named Martin?"

"No," Emily answered after a brief hesitation. "Not that I can remember. But …,"

"Go on," Chris prompted, while staring up at a red light she had stopped at. The afternoon traffic was getting thicker, the closer she got to the Seattle Center.

"There was this one time last month, when we played this game that was supposed to predict who you'd marry. Mine was super lame, but Lisa acted all dreamy about her 'mystery' man, whose name started with an M. I remember, because I teased her about it being our friend Michael, who's had a major crush on her since first grade. But she made kind of a big deal about it *not* being Michael, but refused to say why."

Chris's pulse kicked up a bit, and she had to force herself to focus on the road. "Emily, thanks. This is the kind of stuff I need. If you think of anything else, please call me. It doesn't matter when it is."

"Sure, but Miss Echo ... you need to find him. You need to find the son-of-a-bitch that did that to Lisa!"

Chris didn't get a chance to make a promise she might not be able to keep, because the phone abruptly went dead. A honk from an impatient driver notified her of the green light, and she sped through the intersection.

Pulling over at the next parking lot she passed, Chris then riffled through the papers spread around on the front passenger seat. Finding the one she was looking for, she studied the address before pulling back out onto the road. Turning at the next corner, she drove past the iconic Space Needle before eventually making her way to I5, where she headed north.

Martin Eastabrooke happened to live in an

upscale neighborhood in Issaquah, about halfway between Seattle and her own home in North Bend.

While she had a forty-minute commute on a good day, Chris felt it was worth it. She appreciated the city of Seattle, and the job market there, but was most at home in the mountains. Fortunately, you never had to go very far in the state of Washington to find them.

After a brief twenty minutes of highway travel, she pulled off one of the first exits for Issaquah. Hunting down a coffee stand wasn't difficult, and after getting a tall vanilla latte and bagel, she found a far corner of the lot to park in.

Abandoning her favorite lunch, Chris got out of the sedan and went around to the trunk. In it was a complete forensics kit, including a nice Nikon D5500 camera. She stood staring into the open compartment for a full minute, and then grabbed the bag.

She was about to go rogue.

Not that she was necessarily doing anything illegal or wrong. But it most certainly wasn't within the parameters of what she was *supposed* to be doing this afternoon.

Closing the trunk, she convinced herself that just a quick drive-by wouldn't hurt anything. It would be highly unlikely for him to be home that early on a Thursday. She just needed to see where he lived. What kind of house he had, what sort of yard and neighbors. It would help form a more complete picture of the person she was trying to decipher.

Ten minutes later, half of the bagel was gone, and Chris was sitting at a four-way stop sign. Taking a long sip from her coffee, she stared up the tree-lined street. It was an older community, with established yards and handsome homes. The kind you let your kids ride their bikes in without any fear. His house should be a little way up and on the right.

Her pulse quickening, Chris concentrated on controlling her breathing. She couldn't help but feel like she was in the wrong for being there.

At risk of appearing suspicious, she finally accelerated, with the plan to first roll past at a normal speed, before finding somewhere to pull over and quietly observe from a distance. Watching the house numbers, Eastabrooke's was suddenly in front of her before she expected it.

Cursing under her breath when she saw the sedan in his driveway, she quickly looked around the cottage-style building for any sign of him outside.

There was a man standing in the side yard. Gasping, Chris almost sped up, but then she noticed the darker skinned man was wearing obvious work clothes and had a lawnmower. He had to be a gardener. Then, she was past the property, and craning her neck to look back. There was an old, beat-up pickup truck at the curb, with a crude sign that said 'Yard Champions'. It probably belonged to the man pushing the mower.

Turning at the next corner, Chris pulled over under the shade of a large maple tree. Selecting the thinner file at the bottom of the stack, she found the document listing Martin Eastabrooke's vehicle make and model. A 2014 Lexus IS F. It was worth more than what she made in a year. That was definitely his car in the driveway, and since he was supposed to live alone … it also meant that he must be home.

Scratching at her head, Chris then slammed the file back down in frustration. Why would he be home from work? Tapping her fingers on the steering wheel, she considered her options briefly before pulling back out. Making a loop, she then parked just past that same intersection, but facing the other way, towards his house. She was in front of a two-story country style house with an empty driveway, and the shades were all pulled. A for-sale sign was in the front yard, which was another reason she chose this curb space. If anyone got curious, she could easily say that she was a potential buyer. It would even explain the camera.

Opening the large camera bag, Chris selected a telephoto lens. Attaching it to the body, she then peered through the viewfinder and focused first on the worker's truck. Good. It was a great angle and she could see it clearly.

Next, she pulled back to a wider view and snapped some pictures of the front yard and house. She could tell that the maintenance on the yard was done often, and it struck her as odd. While it was a nice area, it wasn't a gated community with HOA's, or strict requirements. Chris would classify it as upper-middle class, and suspected that families, not single men, occupied most of the 3-4 bedroom homes. It was a small yard, and one that he could have easily managed on his own. Shrugging, Chris filed it away for later contemplation.

Shifting uncomfortably in her seat, Chris hesitated. This was stupid. It wasn't like he'd have a sign on his front door saying, 'I'm a killer'. There were times when she questioned herself more than her superiors. But, she had come to learn to trust her instincts. It didn't always have to make sense.

The car. It was backed in, and as she focused on the windshield and clicked off a few more images, someone walked in front of it, blocking her vision. Yanking her head back, she saw Martin Eastabrooke reach in the sedan briefly before going to the trunk. Chris was a bit disappointed when all he pulled out was a hiker's backpack, but that, along with the hiking attire he still wore, explained why he wasn't at work.

Zooming in on his shoes, she jumped again when her phone rang. Caller ID informed her that it was Andrew, and the guilt she talked herself out of earlier came rushing back full force. Tossing the camera in its bag, she then quickly backed into the driveway of the for sale house, and sped away. So long as she was technically on her way home, she wouldn't have to lie to him.

Chris answered the call on the fifth ring.

Three

Trees rushed past Chris as she jogged along the forest trail, her breath keeping an even rhythm with her feet.

She knew the route so well, that she could almost run it with her eyes closed. Chris had carved the track out of the dirt herself, after carefully choosing the best course through the dense woods. It resembled a deer trail, since her only tools had been her feet, and to the casual observer, it would appear a natural part of the environment. That's how she liked it.

One of the reasons she purchased this

twenty-acre piece of property, was because it backed up against state land. The quaint, two-bedroom cabin that came with it needed a little work, but that didn't scare her away. Or the fact that it was so secluded, that her friends questioned her decision to move out there. She preferred the solitude, when she wasn't at work. She'd learned long ago in counseling that part of being a survivor was choosing not to give in to your fear. She might have taken the mentality a little too far, but for Chris, it was all in or not at all.

Dodging a low-hanging branch, she then sidestepped a large root and hopped over a log. Smiling, Chris picked up speed. This was her favorite part of the course, where it dipped down into a ravine and followed along a small creek. The forest felt magical here, like a scene ripped from a medieval tale. It was also the most challenging section, with plenty of deadfall and rocks to scramble over and around.

Physical fitness had always been an important part of Chris Echo's life. While she'd never been described as skinny, due to her height and solid frame, she'd come to accept and appreciate having an 'athletic' build. She was strong for a woman, and it was one of the reasons why she had excelled while at the police academy. The challenge of her obstacle course in the woods was a perfect way to keep fit.

Slipping on a moss-covered boulder, she almost went down, but managed to grab at a nearby trunk and stop herself. Laughing, Chris pushed even harder, so that she was almost sprinting by the time she began to cross a large tree that had fallen over the creek, creating a natural bridge.

At the midway point, her luck finally ran out. Her foot caught the sharp remnant of a broken branch, sending her flying. Crying out in alarm, Chris frantically flailed her arms, clawing at anything that might give her purchase. She slammed down onto the rough surface hard enough to knock the breath out of her, but frantically wrapped her arms around the trunk in a death grip, keeping herself from falling off and into the ten-foot void below.

Facedown, Chris closed her eyes briefly before pushing herself up onto her knees. Breathing in the earthy smell of freshly disturbed moss on the trunk, mingled with the lighter pine scent of the woods, she took stock. Other than a few scrapes to her chin and elbows, she appeared to be uninjured. Peering down at the jagged rocks below, she realized how stupid she had been.

Cautiously, she returned the way she'd come. Time to get back to reality. Running out here was both a stress reducer and a form of escape. Today, she had to admit it was the later.

Andrew's call unsettled her. He'd offered to come over and help her 'get through the files'. What that *really* meant was, 'I'll come over and we can pretend to be interested in the case. You'll ask me to stay for dinner because it would be the polite thing to do. We'll have a glass or two of wine, and after a couple of failed attempts at seducing you, we'll eventually end up having sex, because there's no denying the chemistry between us.'

She had politely told him no thank you.

The problem was that she wondered if turning him down repeatedly was *really* because of how their friendship started. Hadn't he proven himself to her since then? Maybe it was just a convenient excuse for not allowing anyone to get close to her.

Stumbling again, this time on a rock, Chris stopped and placed her hands on her hips, breathing heavily. She was distracted. The perfect example of *why* she didn't need to get romantically involved with anyone, especially not Andrew. Not only would it complicate her life, but they also had to work together. The department had policies on fraternization, and while it was normally overlooked unless the couple started talking marriage, Chris wasn't interested in muddying the waters at the office.

Taking a step forward, she glanced down to assure that she didn't trip over anything else, and noticed a wrapper off to the side. Instantly irritated, she bent over and picked it up, noting how it was a brand of power bar she didn't eat. Someone else had been on her trail.

Looking around at the trees as though she'd been betrayed, Chris forced herself to admit that while she made the trail, she was currently standing on state land, so anyone could use it. It wasn't that often that another hiker discovered it though, and she'd only seen someone out there one other time.

Shoving the wrapper into the pocket of her running shorts, she tried to focus on the fact that by comparison, the maintained trails of the forestry service would be overrun by people. That she didn't have to drive to a trailhead, and take a chance of having her car getting broken into was cause enough to smile. Let alone the money she saved by not having to purchase a pass--"

Stopping again, Chris took a sharp intake of breath. The forestry pass! It was a sure sign of a hiker, when you saw the orange ticket hanging from the rearview mirror. In Washington State, you were required to purchase the annual pass in order to park at the trailheads. Why hadn't she made the connection before? She was certain she'd seen the distinguishable item in one of the evidence photos of the things inventoried from Lisa's car. And the first possible victim from ten years ago was a forest ranger!

Breaking out into a run, Chris forgot about being careful. Reaching blindly for her fanny pack, she unzipped it and pulled out her cell phone. The only person she could think of to call was Andrew. He was the most likely one to go to

Mick for her and get him to agree to let her come back in tomorrow.

When he didn't answer the phone, she hung up in frustration. Slowing to a walk, she broke down and sent a text message to him, something she rarely did.

Andrew, call me! I have to talk with you ASAP!!!

Slipping the phone back in next to her pepper spray, she began running again. She was eager to get home. Not only was it starting to get dark in the woods, but there was possibly another piece of crucial evidence on the camera. Evidence that could finally provide the link between Martin Eastabrooke and his victims.

Four

Unlocking the front door of her cabin, Chris then tossed her fanny back on the kitchen counter before grabbing some water from the fridge. Guzzling the cool liquid as she made a beeline for the files, she winced at the cold-induced brain freeze.

The main living space was one open room, including the family room, dining room, and kitchen. The back half contained two bedrooms and the bathroom. It was the perfect size for her, and she'd made a number of upgrades, including new tile and wood floors.

First, she grabbed Lisa's file, and started spreading the papers over the dining room table until she found the one she was looking for. "Aha!" she exclaimed, holding it up to the light for a closer look.

Tim Swanson, their lead forensics tech, lined up over a dozen items on a table. He'd commented on how messy Lisa's car was. It was apparently full of school stuff, clothes, old food, and lots of what he called 'garbage'.

One particular photo contained several receipts, a couple of napkins, what looked like homework … and an orange forestry pass.

"Yes!" Chris shouted in triumph, but didn't even pause. Still holding the picture, she grabbed the Nikon that she'd left with her purse on the couch. Sitting down, she turned it on and started scrolling through the thirty or so images she'd taken.

Her headache was ebbing by the time she found the picture she wanted. Zooming in on the windshield, a broad smile spread across her face. Hanging from the review mirror was a square orange piece of paper. Given that Martin had clearly been hiking, it made sense that he also had the pass. He must have removed it when he'd leaned in the front seat, because the item was absent from the two photos she took afterward.

Straightening up, Chris rested the damning evidence in her lap and stared out the nearby window. The woods were so silent and peaceful. While relieved to finally have the one thing that could successfully connect Eastabrooke to the victims, it pained Chris to think that it might have been that same need for solace that led to the women's murders.

Shaking her head, Chris tried to break free of the oppressive emotions. She had a lot of work to do. First, she had to get Andrew on board with helping her convince Martin to put her back on the case *immediately*. She needed access to the evidence collected from the first two murders. She would be looking at it all differently.

There was a very real possibility that the second murder involving Stephanie, Martin's ex-girlfriend, was the anomaly. She may be the only one he had a relationship with, and where she needed to focus. Chris would interview her friends and family again, but this time with new and more pointed questions about her relationship with Martin. Did they go hiking? Where did they go? What trails?

She needed to closely examine the timeframe before the park ranger, Kelly Humphry, was found. Except that Chris would also investigate the campground itself. All of the registered campers, and the reservations. Hopefully, the state kept records for that long.

Lisa's cell phone!

Chris's thoughts sped faster as she got up and began to pace. Kid's lives played out on their cell phones. She needed to go back to right before Lisa started receiving the phone calls from the disposable phone. She would bet that there was a hiking trip right around the same time. Maybe Lisa met a handsome, successful man while out on a hike by herself. She could have been flattered when he asked for her number.

There were probably others.

A predator likes to stalk its prey. If Chris could connect enough of the dots, just enough, she could finally be awarded a search warrant for the home, phone, and computer of Martin Eastabrooke. He might be smart and cunning, but everyone eventually made a mistake.

Encouraged by the thought, Chris finally smiled, and stopped her manic motion in the family room. Looking at the clock on the wall, she was surprised to discover that it was nearly six. Why hadn't Andrew called back yet? Of all the times for him to not pounce on an opportunity to hit on her!

Sighing, she turned to head for her bedroom and a much-needed shower, but a slow prickle of apprehension along the base of her spine made her stop. Cocking her head, she tried to interpret the goosebumps breaking out on the flesh of her arms and legs. Deciding that the cooled sweat from her run was simply making her cold, she stepped into the shadows of her bedroom and reached for the light switch at the same time.

"I didn't think you were ever going to join me."

Jumping in shock at the smooth voice that greeted her, Chris turned to discover Martin Eastabrooke sitting in the middle of her room.

***

Her first instinct was to run. But then Chris saw that in addition to the knife in his left hand, he was also holding a gun in the other. Cringing, she recognized the weapon, and glancing at the empty shoulder harness hanging on her bedpost, confirmed that it was her own service firearm.

"Yeah," Martin said coyly, following where she looked. "Sorry to add insult to, well … *insult*, but it was handy."

"How did you get in here?" Chris demanded, ignoring the bait.

"Does that really matter?" The overhead light cast his jaw into sharper angles, and his grey eyes glinted like steel. "We have much more important things to talk about, don't you think?"

When Chris crossed her arms and stared back unflinchingly, the murderer sighed and slouched a bit in the chair, apparently disappointed with her reaction.

"The window," Martin explained, pointing towards it with the knife. "Given your history Chris, I would think you'd invest in an alarm system."

Paling, Chris chastised herself for showing any outward sign of emotion. It was what he wanted. He was toying with her.

"So you can use the name search feature on Google. Congratulations," Chris replied, trying to keep her voice as even as possible. "But I don't think your concern for my past is why you're here."

Shaking his head, Martin crossed one leg over the other, in much the same gesture as Andrew had earlier that day. The relaxed pose was his attempt to make her fear feel insignificant and his power over her complete.

"You're so quick to judge me, Chris. What happened to you when you were sixteen was extraordinary! That man was responsible for the death of how many girls?" When Chris remained silent, he continued without pause. "But *you* managed to escape. Tell me, why didn't you change your name? The killer is still out there."

Clenching her teeth together, Chris drew upon the hate she kept neatly coiled deep inside on a daily basis. "I chose not to live in fear. To do so would have given him that victory, and I've got a strong dedication to disappointing serial killers." Her voice didn't break, and she never looked away from his cold stare.

"Do you know what the greatest mistake is, between the prey and its hunter?"

An icy fist was firmly grasping Chris's chest, and she struggled to take a breath around it. Martin Eastabrooke was a genius, and when you combined that sort of intelligence with a sociopath, the result was very dangerous. She already knew the answer, but let him tell her nonetheless.

"Underestimating them. You underestimated me, Chris, and I'm afraid that it's going to cost you your life."

"You know that's not true," she snapped, her voice rising slightly. "You're my only suspect in the murder of three women. You'd be the first one they arrested. You'd never get away with it and you're smarter than that."

Chuckling, he uncrossed his leg and stood slowly to his full height of six-foot-two. With his muscular build, he knew he was intimidating, and the move was effective, compelling Chris to take a step back involuntarily. She saw the pleasure at her fear cross his face, and a wave of nausea washed through her. He had a plan. Of course, he had a solid plan.

"I've been watching you for the past three years."

This admission caused such a vile rage to engulf Chris that she nearly gasped. The thought of this monster watching ... *studying* her was unbearable. She felt violated. Her home, where she thought she was safe, was only a façade. Tears threatened to form and Chris drew upon the raw emotions to instead focus on the man in front of her. The only way out of this was to out maneuver him.

"You're a loner, Chris," he continued. "No close friends, no family nearby, and although you're one hell of a looker, no boyfriend. Now tell me, is that because of a deep-rooted fear created by your past, or just that you think you're too good for anyone?"

While he was talking, Chris consciously made the switch from defensive to offensive. In order to get out of this alive, she was going to have to fight. There was another gun under the seat cushion of the sofa. If she could draw him out into the other room, she might be able to reach it.

"I haven't met anyone interesting lately," she answered casually. *Gotta keep him talking.*

A low buzzing sound from the other room began, making Chris jump. It had to be Andrew trying to call her back.

"Expecting a call?" Martin asked, motioning towards the kitchen with the gun.

"Work. They like to keep close tabs on me." The buzzing stopped, and the silence it left behind felt final.

"I can understand that. I'll bet they didn't even know you stopped at my house this afternoon." Titling his head a little, the crooked grin indicated that he already knew the answer. "That was a rookie move. I was a little disappointed in you. But I suspect you were getting a little desperate, and I *did* slip up, didn't I?"

Chris's face burned red from humiliation at how clearly this man had been ahead of her every step of the way. Never again would she make such obvious mistakes. He was right; she did underestimate him.

"None of that really matters though," he stated, waving the gun at her. "Because you see, this has all gotten to be too much for you. This investigation has stirred up emotions you're unable to deal with. You're alone, depressed, overworked, and unable to sleep. It will be perfectly understandable when your suicide is discovered."

Chris winced when she thought back to the text she sent Andrew. It would play right into his scenario.

"My only dilemma," he continued, taking a step towards her, "is how you would do it. Women don't usually shoot themselves. However, you *are* a cop, which puts you in a different class of women, so I think it'll work.

The casual manner with which he discussed her murder was unnerving. Chris had interviewed sociopaths before, but this went beyond anything he'd ever experienced. She was struggling to come up with something to say to him. Playing to his ego wouldn't work, since he didn't care what other people thought. He had no empathy, no sense of guilt or remorse. The only thing she'd been able to determine was that her fear gave him some sort of pleasure. Swallowing all of her pride, Chris did the only thing she could think of to stall him.

"Please," she begged, cowering slightly and retreating several steps beyond the entrance to the bedroom. "I don't want to die."

His handsome features transformed into something reminiscent of a hungry wolf as he advanced on her, and Chris almost wished that she could take the comment back. But it was working.

Throwing the knife behind him, Martin reached out and grabbed her right wrist, yanking her towards him. With her face turned upwards mere inches from his, the madness was clearly visible, as if the mask he normally wore had been torn off.

"We all have to die," he snarled, his breath hot on her mouth.

As he shoved her to the floor, next to the couch, there was a sudden knocking at the front door.

Five

It was horrible timing.

Chris was just reaching for the Kymber .45 that was stashed under the couch cushion, hiding the motion by using the couch to try to pull herself back up. But the insistent pounding on the door compelled Martin to silence her before she could call out.

A crushing weight drove her back to the floor, as the killer launched himself at her, wrapping his free hand around her mouth from behind. The cold barrel of the Glock was pressed to her temple, prompting her to stop the natural urge to resist.

"Shooting you now means I'll have to make you disappear, instead of staging a suicide," he whispered, his face nestled intimately with her own. "It would mean a little more work for me, but that's okay. I'm flexible. However," he continued, pulling back harder on her mouth and forcing her into an obscene, backward embrace, "I would rather not bury *two* bodies. If you value whoever is at that door, you won't do anything that would cause them to come inside. Understand?"

Nodding vigorously, Chris tried to think clearly. Who could it be? She rarely had guests, and they were almost never uninvited.

"Chris! Chris, I know you're in there. Answer the door!"

Tensing, Chris was both relieved and concerned to hear Andrew. He probably thought her text meant she'd changed her mind about his offer to come over and help. He must have already been on his way to her house when he returned her call. Would he try the door? She didn't think she'd locked it when she came in from her run, because she'd been in such a hurry to find out if her hunch was right.

"Who is it?" Martin demanded of her. The sites on the pistol cut into her skin painfully.

Did he know who Andrew was? Searching her memory, Chris didn't think that he'd been around the two times she interviewed Eastabrooke. His claim to have been stalking her may or may not be true. Even if it were, she and Andrew had rarely spent any time together outside of the office or crime scenes. Odds were that he wouldn't have a clue that Andrew was a CSI.

"My neighbor!" Chris spat, hoping she sounded convincing. "He's been hitting on me since I moved in here three years ago."

Just go away, Andrew! Chris thought. She'd rather take her chances with Martin Eastabrooke on her own, without dragging her partner into it.

But as Martin hauled her to her feet and turned her to face the door, the doorknob rattled. The question as to whether it was locked was soon answered as the door flung inward. Standing in the entrance was Andrew, a bottle of expensive red wine in one hand. Well, at least her fantasy earlier had been correct; there would have been wine involved.

"What the hell!" he shouted, taking in the scene the way only a trained cop can. His reaction was instant. Dropping the bottle as he simultaneously reached behind him with the other hand, he had his weapon drawn about the same time he completed the exclamation.

While Andrew was quick to take up a defensive position, he wasn't quick to shoot, since Chris was in the way. Martin, however, had no such constraints. Before Chris even realized what was happening, the gun was removed from her head and firing.

The discharge at such a close range instantly ruptured her right eardrum, but she hardly felt it. The shot finally triggered her fight or flight instinct, and the sudden rush of adrenaline coursing through her bloodstream caused several, cascading physical reactions.

Her vision narrowed, blackening at the edges, and through the distant ringing in her ears, she could also hear the pounding of her own heart due to her hearing receding. Her muscles tensed as her pupils dilated, and the surge of energy was almost overwhelming, causing her breaths to come in quick, ragged gasps. Drawing upon her defensive tactics training, Chris sprang like a wild animal at the sight of her friend and partner falling backward from the impact of the bullet.

Biting savagely at the hand placed conveniently in her mouth, Chris snarled around Martin's fingers and reached for the outstretched arm of his gun-hand. Surprise was her only advantage, and she squeezed the pressure points while pulling his arm down into her rising knee.

The solid impact, howl of pain, and falling gun were all satisfying, but short-lived. Chris shoved back against Martin's chest to put space between them while she twisted around, but he was already recovering from the initial countermoves.

There were no rules in a battle for life and death, and his bleeding fist found purchase in her long, thick hair. Her forward motion was painfully stopped, and Chris felt roots rip loose when she continued to twist in spite of the hold. Her success in facing him was met with a punch to the left side of her head, but she must have caused some damage while disarming him, because the blow wasn't hard enough to hurt. Either that, or she was so pumped up on adrenaline that she couldn't feel the full effect.

Before he could land another blow, Chris put her runner's legs to good use and gave a solid kick to his crotch. As his knees buckled involuntarily, she grabbed at her hair with both hands, close to her scalp, and pushed off his chest with her right foot. She lost some more hair, but managed to tear free.

Stumbling away from him, she looked around frantically for the dropped gun. Chest heaving, she absently ran a hand across her face, smearing both blood and spit back with her tousled hair. Finally spotting the weapon under the coffee table, where it had spun away on the hardwood floor, Chris lunged for it at the same time as Martin.

The wooden piece of small furniture shattered under the assault, when both of them crashed into it from opposite directions. Although dazed by the impact, Chris batted the wood aside and ignored the large splinters that pierced her leg.

Her hand landed on the Glock first, and she gripped the familiar stock in her palm. But Martin scrambled on top of her before she could bring it around. Wrapping her up, she still managed to struggle to her feet with him on her back. They ended up in a stance as if they were on the range, and he was trying to teach her how to shoot. Except this was a deadly dance, and Chris was at an obvious disadvantage.

She couldn't let go of the gun.

Grunting in either pain or rage, or maybe both, Martin attempted to pull her arms inward, so that her elbows would end up splayed outward. Chris knew that he would then twist her hands upward, while holding the gun, ending with it pointing up and under her chin.

Time seemed to slow down, while she watched her own hands drawn in closer to her face. Then, in slow motion, she noticed Andrew at the fringe of her narrowed vision, struggling to sit up. The sight of him caused the strangest of thoughts to cross her mind. While he was six feet, she still considered him on the margin of being tall enough to date. At five-foot-ten, Chris had high standards, and if it weren't for the fact that Martin was a serial killer, he would have been the perfect height, due to where his head fell in comparison with --"

Time abruptly rushed back to normal as

Chris explosively threw her head back, shattering Martin's nose. Blood erupted down her back before she even had a chance to stumble forward, released from his death grip.

Swinging the gun around, she continued to back away, toward the open door and Andrew. Confronting him, a sense of both elation and cold terror coalesced within her. Although blood poured down his face and had already saturated the front of his shirt, his teeth flashed white behind the macabre mask.

The sickening, coppery smell of blood mingled with the sweet aroma of the wine when Chris stepped in the puddle on her kitchen floor. Andrew managed to roll onto his side, and clutched at the wound in his chest. It was hard to tell where his blood ended, and the wine began.

"Touché," Martin purred, clapping his hands together slowly twice, then three times. "And the hunter becomes the prey. Tell me," he continued, spitting blood onto her floor. "Did you figure it out yet? Do you know where I meet my girls?"

Shuddering slightly, Chris refused to allow herself to be manipulated by him. "Get on your knees!"

Instead of complying, he took one slow, small step towards her, his grin spreading and turning into more of a sneer. "All I want to do is talk."

All her senses prickling, Chris brought the gun up a few more inches, and took her own, menacing step forward. "I said, on your knees!"

Pausing, trying to gauge her, the sociopathic killer deliberately raised his hands, perhaps having recognized something in her eyes. "You wouldn't shoot an unarmed man, detective," he cautioned.

Tilting her head slightly, Chris was vaguely aware of Andrew calling her name. Ignoring him, she took another step, out of the wine and onto several splatters of both hers and Martin's blood. "You think much too highly of me," she whispered.

The sound of the gunshot filled the room, and as Chris watched his body collapse, she knew she'd never be the same.

THE END

The first, full length Chris Echo novel is out!

Echo of Fear

Chris Echo thought a private island in the South Pacific would be the perfect escape from the terrors of her life as a CSI profiler. But shortly after retreating to the tropical setting, she finds herself trapped in the middle of something far more dangerous.

Kyle Stone is battling his own demons. And it isn't anything a remote luxury island can fix. After a long undercover mission, he and the guerrilla cartel he's infiltrated are traveling to an exchange when a storm washes them ashore. The resort's guests are taken hostage, and he can either keep his cover intact or save their lives. To complicate matters even further, there's a beautiful captive who may just be his salvation.

Each of the visitors to the island arrives harboring different fears, but they are about to confront the ultimate fear of all, a struggle between life and death. In the midst of the turmoil, Chris begins to realize that perhaps death isn't her greatest challenge after all.

About the Author

Tara Meyers resides in the beautiful state of Washington. When she isn't writing, she's out hiking in the rugged Cascade Mountains, or enjoying life with her two amazing kids and several dogs! If you were entertained by this story, you might also like the novels she's written under the pen name of Tara Ellis.

www.ingramcontent.com/pod-product-compliance
Lightning Source LLC
LaVergne TN
LVHW042116181224
799470LV00006B/86